Stinky Santa

Otto Fishblanket

www.geraldhawksley.com

Jingle bells, Santa smells -
he smells of mouldy cheese.
He doesn't wear any trousers
so you can see his knees.

He smells of dirty socks.
He smells of rotten fish.
He smells of boiled cabbage
served up in a dish.

Santa has a dog called Rover
who's as smelly as a drain.
(He's twice as smelly
when he's been out in the rain)

He has a cat called Tiddles,
who really does quite stink.
He smells like a compost heap,
or a blockage in the sink.

Now I don't want to tell you tales,
and I don't want to seem rude -
but I must point out
that Santa's beard is full of food.

There's sausages and bacon
and cake, and pizza, too.
There's peanut butter sandwiches
and other tasty things to chew.

Santa sleeps in his stinky bed
with his stinky dog and cat,
and even when he's fast asleep
he wears his smelly hat.

Here is Santa's helper,
a smelly elf called Drew.
His face is spotty, his teeth are green,
and he smells like week old stew.

Here is Santa's sleigh,
it's rusty and it's old.
It smells of the rats who use it
to shelter from the cold.

Here are Santa's reindeer.
Boy, they don't half pong!
They smell of pickled eggs,
because they eat them all day long.

But something odd always happens
about December every year -
the air is filled with lovely smells
that tell you Christmas time is near.

Candy canes and gingerbread,
chestnuts roasting slow.
Log fires and pine trees,
the promise of fresh snow.

"December time already!"
Santa starts to laugh.
"Why if it's that time of year again -
I'd better have my bath!"

So he fills up his bathtub
and he jumps in with a shout.
Santa has so much fun -
he doesn't want to get out!

At last he's nice and clean!
He makes sure his beard is dry.
Now it's as white and fluffy
as a cloud up in the sky.

He takes Rover and Tiddles to the pet parlo..
(though they really don't want to go).
They get washed and brushed so clean
they could win prizes in a show!

He tips his reindeer off the couch,
to wash the dishes and tidy up the place.
Soon everywhere's looking lovely,
and Santa has a smile upon his face.

As for Drew the Elf -
his teeth polish up quite well!
He can start wrapping up the gifts
now he doesn't smell.

Santa scrubs and cleans his smelly hat,
so it's bright and fresh as new.
He even puts his trousers on!
Now, what else is there to do?

He shakes the rats out of his sleigh
(He's made them a new home in the woods)
Then he gives the sleigh a polish
ready for the Christmas goods.

He hitches up the reindeer
and goes out for a practice run.
He drives straight through the carwash -
"Whee!" He's having fun!

When Christmas Eve arrives he's ready -
He's clean and fragrant, too!
No more stinky Santa -
he's got a job to do!

So on Christmas Day,
there are Christmas gifts all around the tree,
and everything smells Christmassy -
just as it should be.

But when Santa's gets back home,
he's covered in soot from head to toe.
Does he have a bath?
Somehow I don't think so!

He can't be bothered with that!
He jumps straight into his bed -
and soon he's fast asleep
with his grubby hat still on his head!
Silly Santa!
You'll soon be stinky again!

Have a very smelly Christmas
and a stinky New Year!

Santa's Grotto's grotty.
It's door is bent and creaky,
It's windowpanes are cracked
And it's roof is very leaky.

A grumpy snowman stands guard
In a very grubby hat.
His scarf has come undone,
And I think I saw a rat.

The paint is peeling from the porch
And the fairy lights are dim.
Everything seems mouldy -
It's all looking rather grim.

Inside there is a polar bear
With cobwebs in his ears.
It doesn't look like anyone
Has visited in years.

The shelves are completely empty,
You won't find any toys -
No candy, no surprises,
No laughing girls or boys.

The baubles are all broken
And the Christmas tree is bent.
As for the Christmas fairy -
I don't know where she went.

But something magical happens
When it begins to snow -
The fairy lights start to flicker,
And the fire begins to glow.

The snowman straightens up his hat
And a smile lights up his face,
As one by one the Christmas elves arrive
To tidy up the place.

They dust away the cobwebs
From the polar bear,
And the sound of jolly Christmas music
Begins to fill the air.

Soon the Grotto's sparkling,
The windows bright and clear,
As the happy elves sing,
"Soon Santa will be here!"

And from the North Pole
Come Christmas gifts galore!
When the shelves are full
The gifts are piled up on the floor.

Outside the children are arriving,
They are queuing at the door.
The snowman doffs his hat,
The polar bear waves his paw.

"Come in," call the elves, "Come in,"
"Santa's on his way!"
"The grotto's looking wonderful!"
All the children say.

The lights are brightly twinkling,
It's cosy as can be -
And look! The Christmas fairy
Is back a-top the tree!

Santa arrives at last,
Bursting through the door.
"Ho, ho, ho!" he laughs,
"What are we waiting for?"

"Welcome to my Grotto," Santa says,
"Christmas has officially begun!"
"Hooray!" cry all the children,
"HAPPY CHRISTMAS, EVERYONE!"

All too soon the day is over,
The happy children go on their way,
And Santa's Grotto is closed up again
Until another day.

But Santa slips back in
(He'd left behind his hat).
"Oh, and one more thing," he laughs,
"Happy Christmas, Rat!"

MERRY
CHRISTMAS!

Other books by Otto Fishblanket
available on Amazon
in ebook and paperback:
Piddles the Penguin
Mostly Ghostly

Or visit
www.geraldhawksley.com